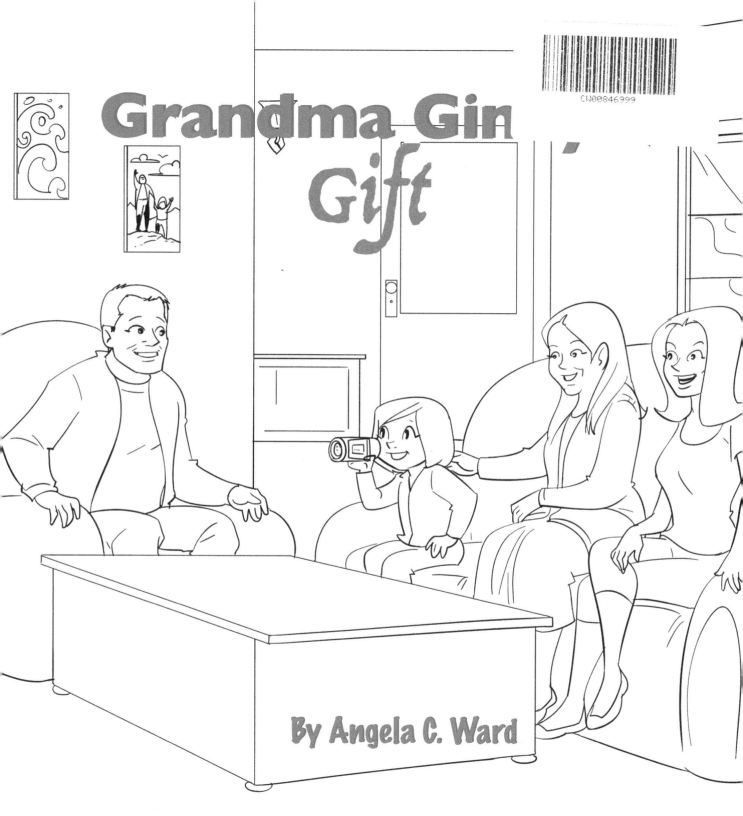

Printed in the United States of America

First Edition, 2022

PAPERBACK ISBN 978-1-0880-4729-3
EBOOK ISBN 978-1-0880-4736-1

Red Pen Edits and Consulting, LLC
P. O. Box 25283
Columbia, SC 29223
www.redpeneditsllc.com

DEDICATIONS

This book is dedicated to my granddaughter, Nia!

Hi! My name is Grandma Ginny. I live in California. I have a granddaughter named Nia that lives on the east coast in North Carolina. I miss her very much.

I miss not being able to hug her and do things with her like go shopping or out to eat. Most of all, I miss spending time with Nia.

Nia recently had a birthday party, and I was able to talk to her via video phone call. I was happy to see her since I couldn't be there in person. Talking to her and singing "Happy Birthday" with her family was something I would not have missed. Watching Nia blow out the candles on her birthday cake was a special moment for me.

Seeing Nia and her parents, Juan and Mya, gave me so much joy. I wished Nia a happy birthday and blew her a kiss.

Nia opened her presents and was pleasantly surprised by the gift that I sent her. She gazed at it for a moment before taking it out of the box.

Prior to Nia's birthday, I spoke with Juan and Mya concerning things that Nia wanted.

Nia had been asking her parents for a camera since last year, but her parents didn't think that she was ready for such an expensive device.

Nia was sitting at the kitchen table eating her favorite snack: milk and cookies. Juan was reading the newspaper. Out of nowhere, Nia asked, "Can I have a camera?" Mya was curious as to why Nia wanted a camera.

So, she asked Nia, "Why do you want a camcorder?"

Nia paused and said, "I want to be a photographer."

Mya asked Nia, "Why do you want to become a photographer?"

Nia told her mother about when Terry's father came to her class last month during Show and Tell to show them his collection of cameras. Terry said that he wanted to be like his father by taking pictures and filming things. Terry's father demonstrated the camera by taking pictures and recording him as he talked to the class.

Mya asked her daughter, "Why do you want a camcorder?"
Nia said, "I want to see the world through another lens."
Mya looked at Juan who was sitting at the kitchen table. Juan looked up from reading his newspaper at Mya and smiled. He said to Nia, "Having a camcorder at your age is a big responsibility. It's a very delicate piece of equipment."

Hearing this saddened Nia.

Juan told Nia, "Your mother and I will buy you a camera that is less expensive and see how well you take care of it. We'll upgrade your camera as you mature and show us that you are responsible."

Nia smiled, threw both of her hands in the air and shouted, "Yes!"

Now that Nia was getting a camera, she couldn't wait to share the news with Grandma Ginny, Mya's mother. Juan, Mya and Nia went to a camera store that sold all kinds of cameras.

Juan talked to one of the associates that worked there about a camera that was age appropriate for a seven-year-old.

The associate showed Juan and his wife a few beginner's cameras for Nia's age. Juan called Nia over to choose which color camera she wanted. Nia picked pink. She said, "Pink is my favorite color."

Nia's parents purchased the camera and took it home to give to Nia.

Mya reminded Nia to be careful with the camera. Her father said, "If you show us that you can be responsible with this camera, then for your 9th birthday, we'll consider upgrading you to a better one."

Then Nia asked, "Can I call Grandma to tell her that you and mommy bought me a camera?" Juan smiled, nodded his head and said, "Yes."
Nia called her Grandma and told her the exciting news. "My parents bought me a new camera. And if I am responsible with this camera, they promise to get me a better one for my 9th birthday."

"That's great news, Nia!" said Grandma. "Now, show your parents how responsible you are by taking care of your camera. Remember Nia, your camera is not a toy."

"Nia, you have to be careful with your new camera. Think of your camera as if it is a baby. When you hold a baby, you have to be very careful."

Nia told Grandma Ginny, "I will take good care of my camera as if it is a baby." Grandma Ginny and Nia laughed.

I asked her parents, Juan and Mya, to let me buy her a camera for her birthday. They told me it was okay to buy one since she did a great job taking care of the camera they bought.

For Nia's birthday, I bought her a Rechargeable Mini Digital Camera with a case. I loved the look I saw on her face when she opened the box, looked inside and saw a new camera. This was the perfect gift as a reward for being responsible with the camera her parents gave her last year. It warmed my heart to hear from Nia's parents that she was responsible with her first camera.

Nia said, "Thank you Grandma! I love you very much! Thank you!"

I said to Nia, "Take plenty of pictures and send some to me so I can see how beautiful they are."

Nia laughed and said, "I will Grandma."

Nia took her camera everywhere. She took pictures of her parents. At Show and Tell, she demonstrated the camera by taking more pictures and showed them to her parents and Grandma Ginny. The more pictures she took and read about photography, the more she wanted to become a photographer.

A few years have passed and now Nia has several cameras. At the age of 12 years old, she enjoys reading books about cameras and photography and she is on her way to becoming a great photographer.

About The Author

~ Angela C. Ward ~

Angela C. Ward is a mother of five grown children and a child of God. Angela was born and raised in Jersey City, New Jersey where she attended elementary school and graduated from Henry Snyder High School. Angela started writing stories in high school from song titles that she liked. Writing was a part of class work and homework that she took very seriously. Angela sought to make the stories interesting in order to explore her creativity. This was best achieved by writing about relationship songs. Angela's teacher enjoyed most of her writings and wrote nice comments next to the grade. Her teacher always inquired about the origin of the stories that came from the imagination and life events of Angela.

Angela was inspired by God to write. The purpose of this new children's book is to explore her creative space by sharing the love of God. "Grandma Ginny's Gift" is essentially a gift to her granddaughter, Nia. This book is dedicated to Nia and the joy that she brings to the lives of so many.

Lightning Source UK Ltd.
Milton Keynes UK
UKHW050851260922
409453UK00004B/18